Good Masters!

Sweet Ladies!

Good Masters! Sweet Ladies!

Voices from a Medieval Village

✝✝✝✝✝✝✝✝✝✝✝✝✝

Laura Amy Schlitz

ILLUSTRATED BY
Robert Byrd

CANDLEWICK PRESS

Partial funding for the writing of this book was made possible by a grant from the Park School of
Baltimore through its F. Parvin Sharpless Faculty and Curricular Advancement Program.

Text copyright © 2007 by Laura Amy Schlitz
Illustrations copyright © 2007 by Robert Byrd

Musical notation on page 17 from *New Oxford History of Music*, vol. 2,
published by Oxford University Press

Second paperback edition 2011

The Library of Congress has cataloged the hardcover edition as follows:

Schlitz, Laura Amy.
Good masters! Sweet ladies! : voices from a medieval village / by Laura Amy Schlitz ;
illustrated by Robert Byrd — 1st ed.
p.   cm.
Summary: A collection of short one-person plays featuring characters, between ten
and fifteen years old, who live in or near a thirteenth-century English manor.
Includes bibliographic references
Contents: Hugo, the lord's nephew — Taggot, the blacksmith's daughter — Will, the plowboy —
Alice, the shepherdess — Thomas, the doctor's son — Constance, the pilgrim — Mogg, the villein's
daughter — Otho, the miller's son — Jack, the half-wit — Simon, the knight's son — Edgar, the
falconer's son — Isobel, the lord's daughter — Barbary, the mud slinger — Jacob ben Salomon, the
moneylender's son, and Petronella, the merchant's daughter — Lowdy, the varlet's child — Pask,
the runaway — Piers, the glassblower's apprentice — Mariot and Maud, the glassblower's
daughters — Nelly, the sniggler — Drogo, the tanner's apprentice — Giles, the beggar.
ISBN 978-0-7636-1578-9 (hardcover)
1. Middle Ages — Juvenile drama. 2. Monologues — Juvenile literature. 3. Children's plays, American.
[1. Middle Ages — Drama. 2. Monologues. 3. Plays.]   I. Byrd, Robert, ill. II. Title.
PS3619.C43C55 2005
812.6 — dc22   2003065256

ISBN 978-0-7636-4332-4 (full-color paperback)
ISBN 978-0-7636-5094-0 (black-and-white paperback)

11 12 13 14 15 16 BVG 10 9 8 7 6 5 4 3 2 1

Printed in Berryville, VA, U.S.A.

This book was typeset in ThrohandInk.
The illustrations were done in ink and watercolor.

Candlewick Press
99 Dover Street
Somerville, Massachusetts 02144

visit us at www.candlewick.com

For my Park School children, who inspired me to write for them;
for Louise Mehta, who believed I could do it;
for Sharen Pula, who kvelled over each monologue as I wrote it;
and for Mary Lee Donovan, who took a chance
L. A. S.

To Ginger, who loved the book
R. B.

CONTENTS

FOREWORD

This is a part of the book that most people skip. This is the foreword—the part where the author tells why the book exists and why the reader might want to read it.

And you can skip it, if you're in a hurry. Nothing bad will happen if you do, because this is a book of miniature plays— nineteen monologues (or plays for one actor) and two dialogues (for two actors). You can read them in any order you like, following your own sweet will.

I wrote these plays for a group of students at the Park School, where I work as a librarian. They were studying the Middle Ages, and they were going at it hammer and tongs. They were experimenting with catapults and building miniature castles, baking bread and tending herbs, composing music and illuminating manuscripts. I wanted them to have something to perform.

The only difficulty was that there were seventeen children in every class, and no one wanted a small part.

It really isn't possible to write a play with seventeen equally important characters in it. If you read Shakespeare, you'll notice that he never managed it—there are always a few characters that have little to say or do. So I decided to write seventeen short plays—monologues—instead of one long one, so that for three minutes at least, every child could be a star.

I was also hoping to pass on my fascination with history.

When I was a student, I had two ideas about history, and one of them was that history was about dead men who had done dull things. History was dates and governments and laws and war and money — and dead men. Always dead men.

But I also read historical novels. And I adored them. People in historical novels loved, fought, and struggled to survive. They died violently; they were beset with invaders and famine and plague. They wore splendid clothes or picturesque rags. They performed miracles of courage and strength just to get something to eat. It was from novels that I learned that history was the story of survival: even something that sounded boring, like crop rotation or inheritance law, might be a matter of life and death to a hungry peasant. Novels taught me that history is dramatic. I wanted my students to know that, too.

I wrote plays about children because I was writing for children. I say children, but the people in these plays are not all the same age. I imagine them being between ten and fifteen years old — you'll have to decide for yourself how old each character is. Some are the sons and daughters of the nobility; others are paupers. Some of the characters know one another, as they all live in or near the same manor.

The manor is in England and the year is 1255.

That's enough introduction. Turn the pages.

Go forward.

GILES

WILL

TAGGOT

ALICE

MOGG

CONSTANCE

HUGO

OTHO

JACK

E

N S

W

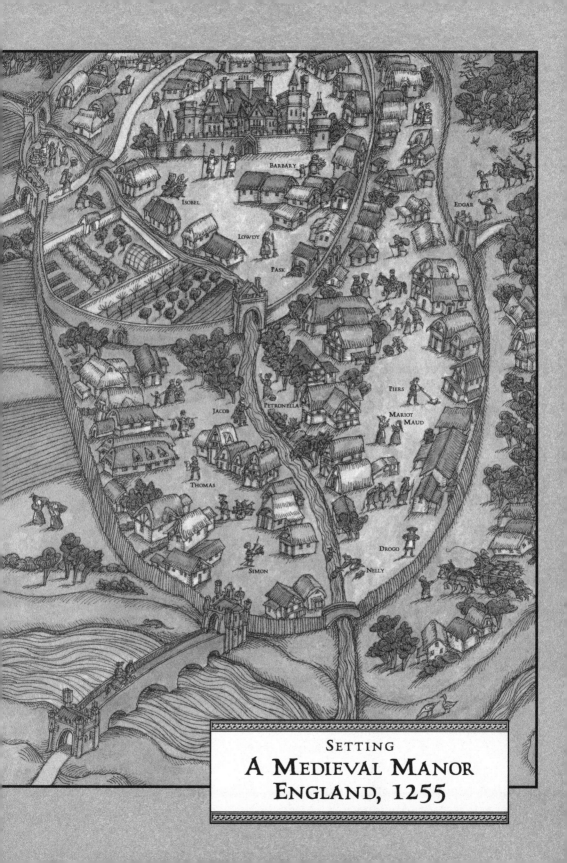

SETTING
A MEDIEVAL MANOR
ENGLAND, 1255

HUGO
THE LORD'S NEPHEW

The Feast of All Souls,[1] I ran from my tutor —
    Latin and grammar — no wonder!
    I ran to the woods, where I saw his tracks —
        this big — and the mud he scratched
        bottom side the trees.
    Followed his friants[2] straight to his bed
        and found it warm.
There was a boar in the forest.

When I went back, there was my uncle,
    rod in hand, but he didn't strike —
    I told him,
    "There's a boar in the forest."

"Why, then, we'll go hunting! And as for you,
    you'll hunt like a man, or be flogged like a boy.
    Help kill the boar, and I'll give you the kidneys —
    turn tail and I'll have the skin off your back."

That night, I lay and dreamed of the hunt.
    The underbrush stirring. The snort of the boar,
        its foul mouth foaming,
        its tusks like scimitars —

those tusks can slice a man, groin to gorge —
    but that's not the worst:
the man that dies from the wound of a boar
    loses his soul, and burns in hell.

Dawn came. We mounted. Long before noon
    the dogs caught the scent, and the hunt was on.
Two relays of hounds, squealing most sore —
    the third was faint with fatigue.

I could smell my sweat, rank with fear,
    and then — it was like my dream —
the underbrush moved, and the sticks shattered.
I saw it — bristling, dark as the devil,
huge as a horse — and my bowels turned to water.

My uncle dismounted
    and I did the same.
My legs were like straw,
    but I walked.
Mouth dry, palms wet,
    one hand forward on the spear
    and one foot ahead
        (to fall would be death).

It charged — my uncle lunged
    and I behind him — thrust! —
    felt the spear pierce.
    Braced myself — end to armpit — shoved.
    It took a long time,
the dogs keening and the boar struggling —

blood on the grass —
but I stood my ground.

At last it was over, and the brute lay still.
    I almost wept:
    the joy of it, and the terror.
        I gasped like a fish, let my head fall back:
        the green leaves swam in the sky.

He kept his word. Right there in the wood,
    we kindled a fire and butchered the boar.
    The kidneys were mine, gleaming with fat.[3]
        He clapped my back, and called me a man.

But dark of the night, I hear that sound —
    sweat in my sleep, and my spear
        slips through my hand —

I dream that I'm back in the wood with that boar.

TAGGOT
THE BLACKSMITH'S DAUGHTER

Nine days it's been since the Maying,[1]
  and I am restless yet.
  Mother hasn't seen it,
  nor Father, nor Robin —
  only the horses know.

It was May Day, and the others
  (even Father and Mother, at their age!)
  set off for the woods,
      wanting bluebells and cowslips
      and kissing under the trees.
        I used to go —
      when I was little, I liked to pick flowers
        and peek —
      but I'm older now —
        my friends have sweethearts.

There's no one for me, and I know why.
  I'm too big. Father says
      his father was a giant of a man —
      somehow his size came down to me.
There's something else. I've stared into the Round Pool,
  and it's hard to tell —
  the water's never still —

but I think I'm ugly. Big and ugly
and shy in the bargain. Mother says
I'll likely not marry at all.
"It's a world of trouble you'll save yourself,"
        says Mother, "childbearing and child dying."
            And no doubt she's right.[2]
I always weep when the hogs are slaughtered.
I'm not strong enough to bear and lose.

"My fine big girl." That's Father.
    He taught me the work of the forge,
    and even Robin admits
        there's no one better to quiet a horse.
        I lay my big hands on them,
        and feel them trembling —
I know how they feel.
        They're like me: big and timid.
So I breathe sweet peace to them —
        not with my lips, but through my fingers —
and they hear me, not with their ears
        but through their skins.

The others went a-Maying, and I stayed behind,
    spinning in the sunshine. The morn was clear as glass,
    and I was happy as a singing bird.

And then he came. Leading his horse
    and the horse limping, head down, head down,
    as fine a horse as I've ever seen —
        a fair gray palfrey, a wondrous horse —
    but I was gazing at the boy.

He had brown hair. Not golden
  like the knights in story,
  and his eyes were dark as rivers.
  The glory was his face —
      the shape of it — I don't have the words.
      He wore a blue cloak,
  bluer than the sky. And in the clasp
  was a sprig of white hawthorn —
      he'd been a-Maying
      and how I hated her,
  the girl he might have kissed.

I was ashamed to be caught staring,
      but I put my hands on the palfrey,
          and he gentled, as they always do.
I ran my hand down the lame leg,
      picked up the hoof, and saw:
          a stone, caught between hoof and shoe —
          a grievous thing.
"Is the blacksmith in?" His voice was like his face,
      proud and courteous.

      My palms were sweating —
          "I can ease him."
  So I led the horse to the forge,
      and the master followed.
I could tell right away he loved his horse.
      I don't know what he thought,
          that a maid should know
          how to shoe a horse.[3]
He may have been startled. I daren't look.

I set to work and my hands were steady.
All the time I was fishing
    for something to say.
        "A fine morning"
        or even "What's your name?"
        But I knew who he was:
        Sir Stephen's nephew —
Hugo, they call him.
        He hunts in these woods —
        he killed a wild boar.
I never did speak. I thought
    if I opened my mouth
    he'd know my whole heart.

When I finished,
    I wiped my hands on my apron
        and he held out a coin — a farthing.[4]
I was sudden bold —
    I reached out my hand and shoved it away —
and then (touching him was what did it)
my face got hot. I could almost hear Robin:
    "Taggot's blushing!
    Lookit Taggot! Taggot's red!"
        I turned and ran
            back to the house,
            crouched down
            with my back to the door.
        I hid my face in my hands —
        I don't know why
        or for how long.

Afterward,
    I went outside,
        back to the forge.
He was gone by then, long gone,
    and it seems a long life —
    I may live fifty years, and not see him again.
    Not close, not to speak to.
    There's a good smith up at the castle.

Thinking that,
    I bent my head,
    and saw, lying on the anvil,
        a miracle:
    that sprig of hawthorn —
    from his cloak, on the anvil.
        If 'twere on the ground,
        it might only have fallen —
    but it was on the anvil.

I picked it up
    as if it was holy.
    I couldn't stop smiling.
        He left it for me.

WILL
THE PLOWBOY

Wheat, barley, and fallow. That's what my father taught me: if you've got three fields, you sow wheat in October and barley in March and let the third field rest. I don't know why the fields have the right to rest when people don't. I only know that's what he told me.

My father's been dead for four years now, but I think of him every day. I used to lead the ox when he plowed. We'd finish the field on the north side of the village, and cross to the west — but that was a long walk, and he'd let me ride the ox. Then the lord gave us a strip in the low field, and that was so far, it took half the day to get there, and I couldn't keep up.

And neither could my father. There was so much walking between the fields, and the strips of land were so small, our harvest wasn't worth a rotten apple. And then there was the work he had to do in the lord's fields — the work he was *paid* to do. Every day he'd bring home three herrings and a loaf of bread — but sometimes the herrings had been dead so long we couldn't eat 'em.

One night he came home late, and my mother ran out and put her arms around him, and I heard her say, "Why, what's that?" And he put his hand over her mouth and led her inside. And under his smock, he had a hare 'most as big as a fox — still warm. He'd killed it with a stone.

My mother cried and she said he'd be hanged, and he told her to clean the hare for supper. So we had fresh meat, and I ate so much I was sick in the night.

He said I couldn't tell anyone, not ever, because that hare belonged to the lord, and we had no right to eat it. And I never did tell, and no one found out. And when he lay dying, he told me to work hard and take care of my mother and sisters — and I promised I would, even if I died of working. I always did everything he told me, and I always will, so long as I live.

"I don't know why the fields have the right to rest when people don't. ..."

THE THREE-FIELD SYSTEM

The three-field system was typical of farming during the Middle Ages. Landowners knew that if they sowed the same crop in the same field year after year, the harvest would be poor. Each year, one field was allowed to lie fallow, and the other two would be planted with a crop different from the one planted there the year before.

Like most peasants, Will's father owned strips of land in all three of the village fields. This made sense in many ways: the labor of working a field that required a lot of plowing was shared, as was the harvest from a fertile field. It also meant that no peasant had all of his land in the fallow field, which would have resulted in starvation every third year.

The drawback of the system was that the peasants had no control over where their strips would be. The lord of the manor was in charge of this decision, and he generally chose the best land for himself. Peasants like Will's father suffered if their strips of land were far apart, because hours of precious daylight were wasted as they zigzagged from field to field.

ALICE
THE SHEPHERDESS

My mother died when I was born,
    so I was suckled by one of the sheep.
    It's made me — my father says —
    more sheep than human,
    which is true.
All my life,
    I've lived with sheep,
    drunk their milk,
    eaten their meat,
    washed their fleece,
    carded their wool.
Now that I'm older,
    I help with the lambing.
    My hands are small,
    which is good,
        if you have to reach inside a sheep.

Jilly's my favorite. She's my sister —
    the same mother gave us milk.
    Most sheep don't care, one way or another,
        but Jilly is sweet of heart.
    I love the feel of her chin
        in the palm of my hand.
    I love the smell of her on my fingers.

It was last spring
      that I wakened
      and knew something was wrong.
"Jilly, what's amiss?" and she only stared
      with the blank, dark eyes of a beast in pain.
      I walked behind her, lifted her tail,
      and saw the head of a dead lamb
      sticking out between her legs.
She'd been struggling
      to push out that lamb
            God knows how long, and me lying asleep.

I rubbed goose-grease on my hands
      and reached inside —
            she was bone dry.
      I know I hurt her, dragging out that lamb,
      and she lay on the ground, as motionless as death.
I called the old shepherd, and made him look at her.
      He said she would die.
      "She's given up," he said. Sheep
            don't fight.
      That's why they need shepherds.

I started to cry, and Old Ralf saw.
      "There's one thing," he said.
      I wiped my nose on my sleeve. "What's that?"

"You might try singing. No one knows why,
      but sheep fancy music. They do."[1]

So all that day
    and all that night,
    I stayed by Jill
    and sang:
        "God restore thee, thou heavenly sheep,
        Hark to my music and heal in thy sleep."[2]

It was really a song for the Virgin Mary
    but I changed the words.
    I sang it over and over
    and the stars came out —
        "Do not forsake me, my sister, my sheep,
        Slumber ye gently and heal in thy sleep."

I stroked her fleece
    and felt her chest a hundred times,
    to see if she was breathing.
        The moon crossed the sky,
    there was dew on the grass,
    the morning star rose,
    and I sang:
        "Best of all in the flock that I tend,
        My lamb, my Jilly, my sister, my friend,
        My lambkin Jilly, thou heavenly sheep,
        Lullaby, lully, and heal in thy sleep."
I sang until my voice was hoarse,
    and I was shivering so hard,
    I couldn't go on.
Then I wrapped my arms around Jill,
    lay down by her side,
    and slept.

I must have slept well,
      because she got away from me.
When I opened my eyes,
      the sky was full red
      and Jill
            was standing up,
                  cropping her grass.[3]

GOD RE-STORE THEE, THOU HEA-VEN-LY SHEEP,— HARK TO MY MU-SIC AND HEAL IN THY SLEEP.

DO NOT FOR-SAKE ME, MY SIS-TER, MY SHEEP,— SLUM-BER YE GENT-LY AND HEAL IN THY SLEEP.

BEST OF ALL IN THE FLOCK THAT I TEND, MY LAMB, MY JIL-LY, MY SIS-TER, MY FRIEND. MY

LAMB-KIN JIL-LY, THOU HEA-VEN-LY SHEEP,— LUL-LA-BY, LUL-LY, AND HEAL IN THY SLEEP.

Thomas
The Doctor's Son

My father is the noble lord's physician,
And I am bound to carry on tradition.
With every patient that my father cures,
I learn more medicine. Ordinary sores
Will heal with comfrey, or the white of an egg.[1]
An eel skin takes the cramping from a leg.
I know five kinds of fever,[2] and four humors,[3]
Bloodletting, and the way to feel for tumors.

I know the stars and movements planetary.[4]
With one whiff, I can sniff out dysentery,
And also, I am practicing the way
To soothe my patients—and to make them pay.
They swear at us when we demand our fee,
But what man can afford to work for free?
A healthy man is careless with a bill—
You have to make them pay when they are ill.

When first you see a sick man, feel his brow
And say, "You should have called me before now!
If given time, I vanquish all complaints,
But as it is, we'll have to ask the saints.
Make sure you pray, and that your heart is quiet,
And think of ways to simplify your diet—

That trencher full of venison I see
Is much too rich! Just hand it back to me!"

After the prayer, let the patient rest,
And tell his family, "I will do my best
To fight this sickness, but I fear his fate—
It may be that you called me in too late."
Then shake your head, look serious and wise—
This sort of talk protects you if he dies.
If he recovers, it was all your skill
That brought him back to life. And that's better still.

Constance

The Pilgrim

I am a pilgrim to Winifred's well,
For Saint Winifred's well will heal me.
When I come back, I will have no need
Of a heavy cloak to conceal me.[1]
> Though I was born crookbacked,
> crippled, and fell,[2]
> I will be cured at Saint Winifred's well.

Saint Winifred was a beautiful maid,
And the evil Caradog[3] desired her.
He sought to seize her against her will
But her love of God inspired her.
> And when she refused him, full of dread,
> He took up his sword, and smote off her head —

But there was the miracle! Winifred's blood
Was crystal clear and flowed like a wave.
The good earth opened. The evil Caradog
Was swallowed unshriven,[4] sucked into his grave.
    And Winifred's neck went back to her head
    Though she had the scar always—or so it is said.

But though she recovered, the magical spring
Comes forth clear and clean to this selfsame day,
And so, though my journey be long and hard,
I will kneel by the shrine of the well and pray,
    For a hunchback's life is a life of scorn.
    I have known more sorrow than tears can tell.
    There are times when I wish I had never been born,
    But I will be healed at Saint Winifred's well.

"I will kneel by the shrine of
the well and pray."

MEDIEVAL PILGRIMAGE

Like many medieval pilgrims, Constance believes that her prayers will be heard if they are spoken in a sacred place—in this case, by a holy well. During the Middle Ages, thousands of pilgrims traveled to pray in the presence of a saint's body, or close to the spot where a saint had been martyred. The physical remains of a saint—even a fingernail or a lock of hair—were believed to be charged with miraculous powers.

I have simplified the story of Saint Winifred, leaving out her uncle, who clamped her head back onto her neck. Saint Winifred recovered from her decapitation and became an abbess. She died around 650 A.D. Her shrine is in Holywell, Wales, and pilgrims still go there to pray. During the Middle Ages, the journey from England to this remote site was a long and difficult one, but that didn't stop people from going. Medieval travelers were a hardy bunch, and sometimes walked hundreds of miles in order to atone for a sin or pray for a miracle.

Medieval sites were often associated with holy springs or wells that had been considered sacred in pre-Christian times. The springs were credited with many miraculous cures. In the case of springs rich in mineral salts, the cures are easily explained: the salts would help to clean and dry up skin infections. Hot springs could ease the pain of aching joints or torn muscles. Other cures are harder to account for, but that's beside the point: medieval people did not share our need to understand the world scientifically. They were convinced that water from a shrine or relics from a saint could cure disease—and it may well be that these "faith cures" were as reliable as the hodgepodge of astrology and folk medicine practiced by medieval doctors.

MOGG
THE VILLEIN'S[1] DAUGHTER

My father died last winter —
     also the chickens. Choked themselves[2] —
thrashed and turned sick, after all the trouble I had
plucking their grass and cleaning their muck
        and not one egg. What was I saying?

My father died,
     lay down with fever, and at first I was glad,
     may God assoil me. "He can't lift his hand,"[3]
        I thought, "while he's sick in the straw.
        Not to me, nor Mother, nor wee Jack."
     But then he grew worse. "Mogg," says Mother,
        "you'll have to take the grain to the mill."

I took that great sack, but the mill wasn't turning.
     The kingpin was broken. I waited eight hours,
        knee deep in slush, to grind my meal
        and give the lord his share.

That's the law. You have to grind at the lord's mill[4]
        unless it's broken a day and a night.
I waited, cursing under my breath
     till they fixed it —
        they ground my corn, and took their cut.

I trod home, with my shoes soaked
and my teeth chattering —
by the time I got home he was dead.

I prayed for him. He wasn't a good man,
always ale-drunk — Mother can only see from one eye.
He beat Jack, and the lad is a half-wit.
But he was strong, and canny with his pennies:
somehow he saved up enough for a cow —
Our Cow.

We call her Paradise — a good red-brindle
not six years old, and strong enough to plow.
Sweet-breathed, sweet-tempered, and bonny.
Jack and I slept with her all last winter —
her body was warm and her dung patched the roof.
A calf for the spring, and milk for the market:
Paradise.

Then Mother tells me: the lord has his rights.

Heriot,[5] they call it. When a man dies,
the lord has the right
to the best beast he had.
"It's his right," she said, but I paid her no heed.
For sooth,
I could have killed Father for dying.

He came early.
A dapple-gray horse, and a ring on his finger.
Pinches his nose when he enters our hut.

Peers at our livestock, fishy-eyed.

I didn't say a word. I was staring
    at the cow in the straw. Not our cow, but Tam's —
Tam Bywater's cow —
        mangy, ribs showing, and breathing like bellows,
a beast not worth the price of its hide.

And Mother is scraping and fawning,
    "If you please, sir . . .
begging your lordship's pardon."
There's Mother, so meek, and blind in one eye,
    her hair falling out, and her shift full of holes —
    making a fool of his lordship.

So. He took the best of the pigs —
    I'd have chosen the same, in his place.
We curtsied. Mother kissed his hand,
    and we watched him ride off,
    and waited till dark,
    to take back Paradise.

OTHO
THE MILLER'S SON

Father is the miller[1]
As his father was of old,
And I shall be the miller,
When my father's flesh is cold.
I know the family business —
It's been drummed into my head:
How to cheat the hungry customer
And earn my daily bread.

Oh, God makes the water, and the water makes the river,
And the river turns the mill wheel
   and the wheel goes on forever.
Every man's a cheater, and so every man is fed,
For we feed upon each other,
   when we seek our daily bread.

My father is a hard man,
Muscular and stout.
He swings a heavy cudgel
Whenever he walks out.
My grandfather was like him
A man of gain and sin:
They found him in the millpond
With his skull bashed in.

Oh, God makes the water, and the water makes the river,
And the river turns the mill wheel
    and the wheel goes on forever.
I used to wonder why the peasants hated us so strong.
They think we pick their pockets —
    and they're not far wrong.

Flour in the flour sack,
Vermin in the flour.
Peasants waiting by the mill,
Hour after hour —
They curse us as they stand in line,
Enjoy their little talk.
My father grinds their flour
And replaces it with chalk.[2]

Oh, God makes the water, and the water makes the river,
And the river turns the mill wheel
    and the wheel goes on forever.
When you think about the matter,
    it's as good as any sermon,
For the villeins feed the miller,
    and the miller feeds the vermin.

When I was only four years old,
Still babyish and unsteady,
I tried to play with common folk[3] —
They hated me already.
They knew I was my father's son —
My father serves the lord.
One day I'll show them hating me
'S a thing they can't afford.

Oh, God makes the water, and the water makes the river,
And the river turns the mill wheel
    and the wheel runs on forever.
There's no use in looking back,
    for here's the truth I've found:
It's hunger, want, and wickedness
    that makes the world go 'round.

For every man's a sinner,
And he wants his neighbor's grain.
The peasant moves the boundary stone
And steals the lord's demesne.[4]
The miller steals the flour,
And the baker steals the bread.
We're hypocrites and liars —
And we all get fed.

And half the world's a-thieving,
    and the other half's a-crawling.
The Mouth of Hell is gaping wide,
    and all of us are falling.
The Judgment Day is close at hand,
    the hellfires are burning.
There's no way to retrace our steps,
    the mill wheel's turning —

For God made the water, and the water makes the river,
And the river turns the mill wheel
    and the wheel goes on forever.
My father used to beat me sore —
    I've learned that life is grim.
And someday I will have a son — and God help him!

JACK
THE HALF-WIT

Lack-a-wit
    Numskull
        Mooncalf
           Fool.
That's what they call me.
That's what they yell in the village
    when I walk through.

I don't say back.
    I'm waiting
        till I get big
        and can hit hard.

My sister, Mogg, says, "Don't listen to them.
    You're no fool —
    can't you milk the cows
    and gather the eggs?"

And I can.
    I can milk as well as anyone.
    I can always find the eggs —
        more 'n Mogg.
    I watch the hens —
    I see where they go.

Father used to say
      I was good for nothing else,
         but Father died,
         and we don't miss him.

Now it's just Moggy
    and me, and Mother
    and the beasts,
       which is good.
       Heaven must be like this:
Jesus, and his Mother,
       and the dumb beasts,
       and angels fluttering 'round like birds.
Nobody ale-drunk,
       nobody yelling,
       or hitting
       or jeering "Lack-a-wit."
       Just friends.

I have a friend
    Moggy doesn't know. She hates him.
       Otho, the miller's son.
       She says he's a thief,
       but I never saw him steal.
They hate him, too,
       the other boys. When they see him
       they whisper
       and snicker
         and throw rocks.

One day last winter
I was hunting the eggs.
He was under the hedge,
    crouched down, crying.
His nose was all bloody,
his eye turning black.
He turned his back
so I wouldn't see,
but his shoulders were shaking
    so hard.

I knew what to do,
    because of Father.
There was still ice
    under the trees.
I clawed up a handful,
    and laid it against his face
    gently,
    and I said what Mogg always says:
        "It'll get better,
        it'll get better,
        it'll get better."

He made a noise
    like a bull being slaughtered
and I cried, too.
I told him he could have my eggs,
    all three.
He didn't answer,
    just kept making that noise,
    his mouth open so he could breathe,

his face all blood and tears and snot.
I stayed by his side till he stopped.

After that day,
    he's been my friend,
    He doesn't speak,
        he doesn't smile,
            but he hasn't forgotten,
            and never joins in
        when the other boys shout:
            Lack-a-wit
                Numskull
                    Mooncalf
                    Fool.

SIMON
THE KNIGHT'S SON

My lord grandfather fought in the Crusades
    with Richard the Lion-Heart.[1] He told me tales:
    how he spitted Saracens upon his lance,
    cleaved them in twain, slashed open their skulls,
    to save the Holy City.

My father, also, was a knight. We had to sell
    some of our land—we *had* land then—
    to pay for his weapons, armor, a horse.
My father came back home a year ago,
       half-starved, horseless, on one leg.

Ever since I was four or five years old
    I knew I'd be a knight. I could see myself,
    a brawny stallion between my knees,
    riding into battle.
    I would fight
       for widows and orphans,
       Christ and His church.
    I would be
       valiant, open-handed,
       frank, and pure of heart,
       courteous—the soul of chivalry.

I would ride into battle,
    slash — cut —
    left — right —
    sharpen my sword on the Saracen's throat —
    crush the bones of the heathen horde —
    all for the glory of Our Lord!

Except there is no money, and my mother
    says I have to be a monk[2] — read Latin and pray,
    scourge myself, and sing at every Mass —
    and cross myself a thousand times a day.[3]

"All for the glory of our Lord!"

A LITTLE BACKGROUND
THE CRUSADES

The Crusades were a series of wars that took place between 1095 and 1272. They were "holy wars"—that is, wars fought for what was considered a holy cause.

We have already mentioned that medieval Christians were fond of going on pilgrimage. The holiest pilgrimage of all was to Palestine, now Israel, where Jesus Christ lived and died. Pilgrims paid homage to Christ by visiting Bethlehem, where He was born, and Jerusalem, where He met His death. Jerusalem was also a holy city for Jews and Muslims, and had been an Islamic city since the seventh century. Its Muslim inhabitants were tolerant of Christians and allowed Christian pilgrims to visit their city.

In the eleventh century, Palestine was invaded by Turks from central Asia. When they captured Jerusalem, they were less hospitable: Christian pilgrims entering Jerusalem could expect to be killed, tortured, or sold into slavery. The same Turks also attacked Constantinople, and the Holy Roman Emperor asked the Pope for help.

The Pope, Urban II, called for volunteers to "free the Holy City" from "the Saracens"—a generic name given to all Islamic peoples, including the Muslims who had allowed Christian pilgrims to visit Palestine in the first place.

What happened next was a thing no one had foreseen. Everyone—men, women, children, knights, peasants, craftsmen—wanted to go on Crusade. The Holy Roman Emperor wanted trained warriors; instead, he got thousands of volunteers who didn't know where they were going or what they were doing. For the first time in the history of the Christian church, people had been told by the Pope that killing people was not only permissible, but a religious duty. Ordinary people could escape the tedium of their everyday lives, see the world, kill

Muslims, and go to heaven in the bargain. Even the villeins could go: their duty to God was more important than their ties to the lord of the manor. The Pope assured Christians that anyone who died, even along the journey, would have his sins forgiven and earn a special place in paradise.

This struck a lot of people as a good deal, and they swarmed to the Holy Land, often slaughtering fellow Christians on the way. Since the Christians they met spoke unfamiliar languages and wore unfamiliar clothes, the Crusaders assumed they were some kind of Muslims. Jews were also slaughtered as this volunteer army of "Christian soldiers" headed to the Middle East.

The crusading fever even affected children. In 1212, a French shepherd boy had a vision that the Holy Land could be recovered by innocent children. Thirty to forty thousand children from France and Germany set off to Palestine, believing that God would favor their cause because of their faith, love, and poverty. They believed that when they reached the Mediterranean, it would part, like the Red Sea. They were mistaken. Most of them starved, froze to death, or were sold into slavery.

Let me stress two things about the Crusades before I leave the subject. One is that the Crusades were very expensive. The armor in use at the time was chain mail, in which every ring had to be soldered by hand. A trained war-horse was also expensive, and Simon's father was not alone in being bankrupt after the war.

Another thing I wish to stress is that the Crusades were an unholy muddle of political motives, greed, savage brutality, and religious fervor. In spite of this, the Crusades had a sort of glamour that has lasted to this day. It is ironic, but when we say someone is a "crusader," we generally mean he is striving to do something noble: he is trying to improve the world.

EDGAR
THE FALCONER'S SON

Listen now, my sparrowhawk,[1]
The stars are fading. Soon the bell
For Prime[2] will ring. I'll raise thy hood,
Untie thy leash, and fare thee well.
The mews[3] are all but emptied now,
The great birds auctioned, one by one—
One single sparrowhawk is left:
The one tamed by the falconer's son.

And that's thyself. Master Simon's
Off to be a monk, and thou
Must ride his fist to Saint John's[4] Abbey,
Save that I will free thee now.
I will not leave thee to his care.
I know young Simon. I know thee.
I'll loose thy jesses, cast thee off—
Even though they punish me.

'Twas I who stole thee, two years hence,
Climbed to the heights with many a qualm,
Scooped thee from thy mother's nest.
I felt thy heart beat 'gainst my palm.
I was the one who filled thy crop—
I fed thee, stroked thee, day and night.

Thou wast my captive and my child —
All savageness and appetite.

And it was I who gentled thee,
I was the one who drew the thread
That seeled thy eyelids.[5] And for thee
I hungered and forsook my bed.
Long in the night I walked the floor,
Carrying thee upon my glove.
I fed thee dainties — mice and eels,
Adder skin and heart of dove.

But now the manor's bankrupt, failed.
The master's hawking days are done.
The mews are empty, save for thee:
Property of the master's son.
But Simon will not tend to thee.
He would let thee starve and pine —
A callow,[6] shallow, pampered youth.
By law of justice, thou art mine.

And being mine, at break of day,
The hour comes for us to part.
I'll loose thee, Splendid, come what may,
Even though it break my heart.
Neither of us will shed a tear
The moment when I set thee free —
Thy valor taught me scorn for fear.
What care I what they do to me?

"One single sparrowhawk is left...."

A LITTLE BACKGROUND
FALCONRY

Falconry, or hawking, was one of the most popular sports of the Middle Ages. Though hawking had a practical purpose—obtaining meat for the table—this was perhaps less important than the excitement and prestige the sport provided. Large birds of prey were status symbols because they were so expensive. It took time and infinite patience to train a bird for hunting. A falconer like Edgar's father was better paid and of higher social status than a groom or varlet.

The gear associated with hunting birds was artfully made. A bird would require a carefully crafted leather hood, jesses (strips of leather attached to the talons), and a leash, which tethered the bird to its perch. A well-trained falcon might be worth her weight in gold. (I say *her* because female birds were larger and stronger than males.) When a falconer fed his bird, he stroked her with one of her own feathers, often accompanying the feeding and stroking with a scrap of melody: always the same song. This was part of the taming process.

In this monologue, Edgar is gambling that the punishment for setting Simon's hawk free will not be more than he can bear. Though he claims that by justice the bird is his, by the law of the land it belongs to Simon's father, since it was captured on his land. Because tamed raptors were so valuable, the penalty for stealing one—which is what Edgar is doing—could be imprisonment mutilation. Since in this particular case the bird is of little value, Edgar may be lucky enough to get off with a whipping.

ISOBEL
THE LORD'S DAUGHTER

I cannot get this stain
    out of my gown. I have tried
    chicken feathers, water,
    urine, and ox gall[1] —
    and still this mark.

My father will be angry:
    a fine silk gown
    spoilt!
    but it's not my fault.

I passed through the town on my way to the market
    and somebody threw it — a clod of dung.
I saw the boys, but I didn't know which —
I was walking eyes down, as a modest maid should.

Then it hit me. I looked up
    and saw them
    sniggering,
    hiding their smiles
    in their dirty hands.

If I told my father,
    he would see that they all

had a good beating, and maybe I should.
But I cannot but think:
>Only one threw the clod.
>Only one should be beaten.
>>But which?

I cannot take
>the stain from my gown
>or the thought from my mind: They hate me.
>>Why?
>What have I done? With my own soft hands
>>I have given out bread on Lammas Day,[2]
>>From my own purse I give to the poor,
>and in times of war
>>those selfsame boys
>>would scurry like rats
>>to hide themselves in my father's walls.

Yet it is true:
>I am better clad
>>better shod
>>and better fed
>>than those — churls.
And what if I am?
The Lord God
>chose my father to rule
>the same way he chose them to serve.[3]
I do but take
>what they would take
>if the Lord God chose
>to give to them.

I want to forget
    the way they laughed —
        their smiles were so ugly
           I almost feared.
        They were big boys, almost men,
           and I was alone
                except for my maidservant Emmot.
"Never mind, my lady," she says to me.

But I do mind.

My gown is spoilt
    and never again
    will I walk through the streets
    with my eyes cast down.

BARBARY
THE MUD SLINGER

I shouldn't have done it.
I knew it was wrong
    when the muck left my hand —
it was folly and cruelty.
And I wish I hadn't.

I was off to buy fish,
    and my stepmother[1] said
    take the twins. "Why?" said I.
"*Both* of them?"
    Bad enough with one.
    They're strong now,
        leaning their weight
        against my hand,
        dragging me in circles.
    I can only carry one —
        the other hauls at me.
        How should I manage the shopping?

"Just take them," she said, and burst into tears.
    "I want them out of the house. Just take them,
        you hear me?
    There'll be more come Christmas. Six months,"
        she said, and the tears

rained down her face.
"Another babe come Christmas."

I stood there
with my jaw almost touching my knees.
More babies?
        There's the twins, up and running.
        They don't sleep at night.
        They still puke out
                most of what you scoop into them.
                They shriek like hawks all day long.
                The cottage stinks like a midden—
                        baby's mess everywhere.
        More babies?

I wanted to scold,
        but my stepmother sank down in the rushes
                and wailed like a babe herself.
        It's worse for her than it is for me—
                birthing the twins near killed her.

So I took up my basket and snatched up the twins.
        One held by hand,
                the other on my hip,
                we set off for market.

It wasn't easy.
        The twin on the ground
        grabbed the fish from my basket
                and threw it. It landed

by the water trough, and I had to wade
    through the mud to get it back.
The twin on my hip
seemed quiet enough —
till he started to bellow.
I smelled something rank,
    and I felt it,
    leaking down my dress.
I couldn't staunch him —
my hands were full.

That's when I saw her,
    Isobel, the lord's daughter,
        dressed in blue.
    Her hair was combed, sleek as an otter.
    Her veil was snow white.
        She had a servant
            to carry her basket,
            so her hands were free
        to pinch up her skirt,
        and pick her way through the muck,
        daintily, daintily.
    Her lips were curved,
        like the smile of a cat,
        and something got into me —
            maybe 'twas the devil.
    I let go of the twin,
        picked up a handful of
        dung, filth, God-knows-what
        and let fly.

Bull's-eye. But I didn't enjoy it —
    not for more 'n a moment.

    Not after I saw her face.
        She hadn't done anything to me,
    and the smutch of the mud
    against her blue gown —
        the prettiest dress I ever saw.
            I ruined it.

The boys in Shamble Lane[2] laughed.
They won't tell on me. They're my friends.
        I saw her eyes pass over me
            and rest on them. She thought they did it.
I ought to have said —
    something — I'm sorry,
    'twas my doing —
    but my little brother
        picked up something foul
        and mashed it in his mouth.
By the time I got to him,
        pried open his jaws,
        fished it out,
        and bellowed, *"No!"*
            she'd plucked up her skirts to go.
Her back was straight as a knife,
        her head held proud, poor girl.

I was sorry,
    almost to weeping.

On the way home
    I went to church.
    I dragged the twins before the crucifix
        and knelt down, trying to pray
        and keep hold at the same time.
    It wasn't easy. I prayed
        that God would forgive me —
        that the muck would come out of her dress,
        that my stepmother wouldn't die.

It made me think
    how all women are the same —
silk or sackcloth, all the same.
    There's always babies to be born
        and suckled and wiped,
        and worried over.
Isobel, the lord's daughter,
    will have to be married,
    and squat in the straw,
    and scream with the pain
    and pray for her life
        same as me.

And thinking of that,
    I added one more prayer —
        sweet Jesus, come Christmas,
           don't let it be twins.

Jacob ben Salomon
The Moneylender's Son

And

Petronella
The Merchant's Daughter

for two actors

I am
   Jacob ben Salomon,
   son of the Jew.
I come to the stream
   to fetch water.
I avoid the well:
   in our old town,
   there was sickness —
they said
   that we poisoned the well.
Why not?
   Why not blame the Jews?
We paid the fine —
   ten thousand marks —
   bore curses,
   blows,
   spittle, and stones,
   but that, of course,
   was not enough.
There is no such thing as
    enough.

We had to go —
　　pack up our things.
　　Our journey ended here,
　where different strangers,
　different Christians,
　hate us — but they take our money.

I came to the stream.
　On the opposite bank
　was

Petronella,
　the merchant's daughter,

across the stream.

Petronella,
　the merchant's daughter.
I saw the Jew
　across the stream.
My mother sent me
　for watercress.
I saw him there — that Jew,
　the yellow badge
sewn to his cloak,[1]
　those staring eyes.

She picked up a stone.	*I picked up a stone.*
The Christians	*My brother and I*
always	*always*
throw stones at Jews.	*throw stones at Jews*

She picked up a stone.
The Christians
  always
    throw stones at Jews.

I saw her stoop,
  pick up the stone

I wouldn't run
  or shield my face —
  a girl's aim
    isn't much.
I glared at her,
  furious.

I wouldn't flinch.

I picked up a stone.
My brother and I
  always
    throw stones at Jews
      except when they practice
      their festivals
    (which the Pope has
    forbidden,
    God rest him).

He saw me stoop,
  pick up the stone.
    He waited.
  Why?
  Why didn't he run?

He stared at me,

frightened,

but he didn't run.

JACOB:	PETRONELLA:

PETRONELLA:

I thank my God I am a maid
   and not a man
   who must hunt with a bow.
If I were a man
   and I saw in the wood
   white-feathered swan
   or soft-eyed doe,
I could not shoot.
I could not force
   my hand to let the arrow go.

She threw the stone —
   but not at me

skimming

bouncing
   twice
     over the water.

I picked up a stone
   and threw —

I threw the stone —

   over the water
     skipping

   swift and merry

   over the water.
He stared at me.

   one, two, three, four!
Four times it skipped,

bounced like a ball—
I clapped my hands
and saw him smile.
He wasn't really like a Jew.
He wasn't like a Jew at all.

We played there

happily

half an hour,

cast our stones
at the watercress stream.

They skipped,

splashed,

sank.

We laughed together.

Time flowed past us like a dream.

She was different
from the others
though I know
that can't be true.
She was like
a friend, a sister—
not like a Christian,
more like a Jew.

He was different
from the others
though I know
that can't be true.
He was like
a friend, a brother—
more like a Christian,
not like a Jew.

JACOB:	PETRONELLA:

PETRONELLA:

The bell tolled
   for Nones.[2] I remembered
my basket,
   empty.
My mother—
   what would she say
   if she knew
I wasted time in the
   woods with a Jew?

JACOB:

When I heard the bells,
   they seemed to say,
   "She is a Christian—
   an enemy."
I thought of my God.
I thought of my people.
   I turned on my heel
   and walked away.

PETRONELLA:

I stopped and plucked
   the watercress.
When I looked up
   he was gone.

JACOB:	PETRONELLA:
One half-hour	*One half-hour*
I forgot,	*I forgot,*
standing there	*standing there*
in the water's shoal,	*in the water's shoal,*
who she was	*who he was*
and my duty to God:	*and my duty to God:*
I never told a living soul	*I never told a living soul.*[3]

"Why not?
Why not blame the Jews?"

A Little Background
Jews in Medieval Society

During the Middle Ages, life in Europe was very difficult for Jews. The economy was based on farming, but in most countries, Jews were not allowed to own land. They were also barred from the guild system. Most legal transactions were based on an exchange of oaths sworn in the name of Jesus Christ. Because Jews did not believe in the divinity of Christ, they found themselves locked out of medieval society. There were few ways in which they could earn a living.

One way was by lending money to Christians, often at a high rate of interest. The Christians liked being able to borrow money from the Jews, but they hated paying it back and often they didn't. The courts were run by Christians and seldom resolved lawsuits in favor of Jewish moneylenders. That was one of the reasons the interest rates were so high — the moneylender ran the risk of losing his money altogether.

Because they were a religious minority, Jews often served as scapegoats for crimes they never committed. There was a widespread belief that Jews poisoned wells and kidnapped children to use in ritual murders. Pope Innocent IV went on record saying that the Jews were not guilty of these crimes, but the accusations persisted. One reason they persisted was that the lord of the manor could accuse the Jewish community of a crime, find the entire community guilty, and impose a heavy fine. The Jewish community would scrape together enough money to pay the fine, so that people could keep their homes and continue to live under the lord's protection. Sometimes — as in Jacob's case — paying the fine was of no use, because after the lord had pocketed the money, he drove the Jews out of town. In spite of these hardships, most Jews remained faithful to their religion and resisted the pressure to convert to Christianity.

During the Crusades, the prejudice against Jews grew more severe. Christians stoned and beat them with clubs when they were practicing their religion. In his Constitution for the Jews (1199), Pope Innocent III forbade these injustices and added: "We decree, blocking the wickedness and avarice of evil men, that no one ought to dare to mutilate or diminish a Jewish cemetery, nor, in order to get money, to exhume bodies once they have been buried." In other words, it was necessary for the Pope to tell Christians not to dig up Jewish corpses and hold them for ransom.

LOWDY
THE VARLET'S CHILD

Father is a varlet,[1] and the varlet serves the lord.
He feeds and tends the master's hounds
    And takes a fair reward.
I've helped clean the kennels,
    Held the puppies on my knees.
I love the dogs, but God's bones!
    The house is full of fleas!
        Fleas in the pottage[2] bowl,
        Fleas in the bread,
        Bloodsucking fleas
        In the blankets of our beds,
        Nibbling our buttocks
        And the backs of our knees,
        Biting and delighting
        Through the night — those fleas!

My mother died when I was born.
    The house is mine to keep.[3]
It's my fault if ten thousand fleas
    Bite us when we sleep.
I've used bird-lime and turpentine,
    Enough to make you sneeze,
Alder leaves and lavender —
    We've still got fleas.

Fleas with good appetites
Somersaulting high,
Fleas leading chases
Running races on my thigh.
Fleas leaping hurdles—
They're as strong as Hercules.
The master raises hunting dogs,
And we raise fleas.

I'm proud of my father as he cares for dog and brach.[4]
He brings food for the table, and dung for the thatch.
Even when the winter's bad and others starve and freeze,
We've porridge from the kennels—
    But we also have the fleas.
        I'm used to the lice
        Raising families in my hair.
        I expect moths to nibble holes
        In everything I wear.
        I scrape away the maggots
        When they crawl across the cheese.
        I can get used to anything,
        Except for the fleas!

        Fleas between my fingertips,
        Waiting to be squashed.
        Fleas floating dead
        In the water where I washed.
        I itch in the cathedral
        When I pray upon my knees:
        God, You saved us from damnation;
        Now save us from the fleas!

PASK
THE RUNAWAY

I don't know when I ran away. But it was past Eastertide, and before Lammas. Lammas to Michaelmas, and Michaelmas to Christmas. Christmas, Lent, and Easter. It must be nearly a year.[1] Once I've lived in town a year and a day, I'll be free. That's the law.

The worst is over. This past winter, I don't know which was worse, the hunger or the cold. But I knew I would never go back.

My father used to say he wished he'd run away when he was young and had no wife and children. "Once there's mouths to feed," he'd say to me, "you're a slave for life. You work till you drop down dead, just to feed your children." But he never did feed us. It wasn't his fault—a villein only gets what the lord lets him keep, and our lord was tightfisted. Then there was sickness, and my parents died. And I ran away.

I wish I'd kept count of the days since I left. Once I'm free, I can start looking for work. Town work, the kind where you get money, instead of old cabbage leaves and the dregs of the beer. I'll get someone to teach me to make barrels or rope or meat pies. That'd be the best, to work around food.

Someday I'm going to buy me one of those meat pies—one that's hot—and eat the whole thing, all at once. And someday I'll buy new clothes. When winter comes, I'll have shoes on my feet instead of rags and straw. And when it's harvest time, I'll go to the fair and buy a blue ribbon for the girl who works up at the kennels.

She was kind to me last winter. I'd been thieving and doing odd jobs, but the snow had been falling three days and everyone was within. There was nothing to steal and no work to be had. I took shelter in the kennel with the dogs. That's where she found me. She came in with the dog's food, and the hounds jumped up baying, and I huddled by the wall, in the shadows.

But she saw me. The dogs were 'round her, barking, but she looked past them to where I sat shivering. She came over and dipped her hand in the dog's bucket, and held out a handful of porridge. I was so hungry I snatched her hand and gobbled, same as if I was a dog. I gulped down the dog's food and sucked her fingers, and she gave me more. And even as I was eating, I knew how queer it all was, but I didn't care. She was a stranger and stank of dog, but I licked her palm as if it were a golden plate.

She let me stay till the weather thawed. I kept out of sight as best I could. From time to time she gave me something to eat. She told me the names of the dogs. She loves the puppies best — her hands were covered with tooth marks. She looks a bit like a pup herself — she has shaggy hair, and it hangs in her eyes and flops down to her shoulders. Like ears.

Someday I'll go back to her. I'll wear new clothes, and I'll go to the kennels and tell her I'm free. Not a villein, not a vagabond. A free man. And I'll give her a piece of ribbon — blue as her eyes — so she can make herself pretty and tie back her hair.

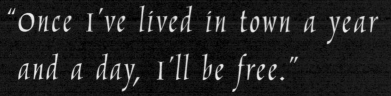

"Once I've lived in town a year
and a day, I'll be free."

TOWNS AND FREEDOM

"Town air makes men free." The proverb has come down to us from medieval times. It is important to remember that the vast majority of people in the Middle Ages were farmers with a limited amount of land. They lived in what we would consider desperate poverty, and they were dependent on the whims of the weather and the good will of their lord.

That being said, not all villeins were as unfortunate as Pask's father. If a villein inherited enough strips of land to support his family, or if he was lucky enough to serve an honest and generous lord, he might live in relative comfort. A villein's fate depended on the land he worked and the temperament of the lord he served. Pask's father was unlucky on both counts.

During the late Middle Ages, the world was changing: towns were growing, and more people were making a living by trade. These townsmen enjoyed a degree of freedom that was unknown to their country cousins. If a townsman suspected that the local miller was cheating him, he could take his flour to another mill. If a shoemaker's shoes were not bringing in enough money, he could make better ones—or cheaper ones—or bellow out the virtues of his shoes in a louder voice.

A villein who ran away and lived in town for a year and a day gained his freedom. This was a bold step to take: it meant risking the lord's pursuit, and losing contact with everything that was familiar. Though Pask has been lucky this far, he may find it difficult to obtain the kind of skilled work he desires. A baker, cooper, or rope maker usually started his career as an apprentice, which meant that the master who taught him had to be paid.

PIERS
THE GLASSBLOWER'S
APPRENTICE

After three years of pumping the bellows
    and stoking the furnace,
    I said to the master,
    "When do I learn to blow glass?"
He stared at me
    with his one blue eye.
    The other was burned in a workshop fire—
    there's a red seam down his face
        where the eye melted shut.
        Once I was afraid of him.
        Not now.
"When I choose to teach you."
    That was all he said.

For the rest of the week,
    I was peevish and slothful.
He knew I was wroth, and once he said,
    "You won't find it easy.
    It's harder than it looks."
But then he said, "Now."
    And I blinked, bone stupid:
    "What now?"
"You wanted the chance to blow glass.
    Now try it."

So I did. I'd watched him a thousand times.
　　I took the iron pipe and held it in the fire
　　　　till it glowed red hot. My hand—
　　　　my left hand, nearest the fire—
　　　　throbbed with the heat, and I felt the sweat
　　　　run down my chest.
I gathered the glass—white hot, glowing
　　and put the pipe in my mouth.
　　　　And blew. And blew—
　　　　but it didn't work.
　　　　　　The glass was stiff, and it wouldn't swell.

I put my thumb
　　on the mouth of the pipe,
　　sucked air—blew out,
　　　　and all this while
　　　　　　the glass is getting colder
　　　　　　　　duller

　　　　　　　　　orange
　　　　　　　　　　blood red
　　　　　　　　　　　mud red
　　　　　　　　　　　　black.

I didn't dare look at him—
　　that one-eyed stare—
　　but his voice was kind.
"Again."

I took the pipe,
　　gathered the glass,
　　sweated—blew—

my cheeks puffed out —
the iron pipe banged my teeth —

I blew like the Angel Gabriel
sounding the horn for Judgment Day.
I felt the bubble start to form —
I'd trapped the air!
I plugged the pipe —
rolled the glass —
twirled it on the marble slab,
and now my right hand burned and ached
and the glass was off — lopsided!

I didn't dare to lift my head
The glass was ruined, but he said,
"Well done!"

Saint Luke,[1] please help me try again,
and keep my master well.
Amen.

MARIOT
AND
MAUD
THE GLASSBLOWER'S DAUGHTERS

for two actors

MARIOT:	**MAUD:**

MARIOT:

None of our father's
  other apprentices
  ever won Father's
  approval like Piers.

MAUD:

Father's taught many a
  boy to blow glass.
We've had apprentices
  year after year.
But Piers
  has the eye for it.

MARIOT:

That's what our father says.

MAUD:

Piers has the lungs

MARIOT:

  and he's hard-working, too.

MAUD:

So Father says Piers

MARIOT:

will inherit the business.

MAUD:

That is, if he marries

MARIOT:

one of us two.

MAUD:

one of us two.

From this point on, the girls are soliloquizing—telling their secrets to the audience. They are no longer telling one story together.

MARIOT:	MAUD:

MAUD:

Marry! God help us!

MARIOT:

Piers never speaks to us.

Nose in the air,
and silent—and rude.

Even at suppertime
  Piers doesn't talk.

He crouches down low
  like a dog at his food.
Both of us hate him.
Mariot's older,
  older than me,
    and the same age as Piers.
If he marries my sister,
he'll get the shop sooner.
I won't be ready
for five or six years.
But Mariot's dear to me.
How can I sacrifice
  her to that
    boy with the
      sticking-out ears?
How can our father,
  be so tyrannical?
Nobody in her right mind
  would want Piers!

MARIOT:	**MAUD:**

Maudie is younger.
Probably Piers
  would rather have somebody
  younger instead —
and Maud is so pretty,
even though Maud is
  the one who put
  all of those
  slugs in his bed.
Piers isn't bad-looking,
  not when he's laughing.
  His hair is uncombed,
  and his clothes are awry.
He'd look a lot better
  if only he smiled,
  but Piers is an orphan —
  he's proud and he's shy.

If I *have*
to wed Piers,
I'll go out
of my mind.

It's not that I like him.
It's just that it's kinder

The way that he scratches,
  the way that he peers
  at what he's scratched
  up —

  and, of course, more refined
  to treat him with

earwax,

courtesy.

grime from his skin.

He's alone in the world,
  and I know that
  he's often been
  lonely.

He's *lousy!*[1]
His fingernails—ugh!

Sometimes when I watch him,
  I'm aware
  of a kind
  of a tug
  at my conscience.
What if I
  befriended him?
  Mended his tunic
  and helped him to tend
  to the burns on his fingers,
  his bedbugs and fleas?
I know what would happen—
my sister would tease.

And then there's his haircut!
The shape of his head!
He looks like a hedgehog.
What maid wouldn't dread
  a marriage with one
  who's so churlish and rough?

MARIOT:	MAUD:
	The truth of the matter
I'm not brave enough.	
	is that Father is thinking
I'm constantly shrinking—	
	of business and profit,
	of shillings and pence.
I should have more courage,	
and follow my conscience.	
However Maud teases,	
I should have more sense.	
	He ought to be thinking
	about his poor daughters.
	Why must we submit
	like lambs to the slaughter?
I ought to tell Maud	
we should both	
hold our tongues.	
	Must Mariot be wed
	because Piers has good lungs?
I must find a way	
to follow my conscience.	
	I must find a way
	to change Father's mind.
Of course I'm too young	
to be thinking of marriage.	
My only thought is to be	
decently kind.	
To marry a man	

MARIOT:	MAUD:
	There's no time to be lost—
is a matter of weight.	
	if I have to accost
	him, I'm going
	to tell Father
	we simply *hate* Piers—
	I'll go down on my knees.
	I'll say please. I'll shed tears.
You share your whole life,	
	I am willing to beg.
your children, your workdays,	
	I'd rather have plague,
your sorrows, your pleasures,	
your ale and your bread,	
	I'd rather have leprosy,
even your bed.	
I must	
think over	
clearly what	
Father has said.	
If I have to be wed,	
then, when all's done and said—	
	I would rather be dead
I'll wed Piers	*than wed Piers.*

NELLY
THE SNIGGLER

I was born lucky. Nay, not born lucky, as you shall hear—but lucky soon after and ever after. My father and mother were starving poor, and dreaded another mouth to feed. When my father saw I was a girl-child, he took me up to drown in a bucket of water.

But here's the lucky part—and 'tis pure sooth. I didn't drown, babe though I was. I took hold with my wee fingers and held to the side of the bucket.[1] And my mother wept, and my father's heart went soft, and he could no more drown me than himself—and they named me Nelly, for Queen Eleanor.[2]

And their luck changed. First my uncle died of the scurvy and we got his pigs. Then the nuns at the abbey hired us to catch eels—and we've been sniggling ever since.[3]

Do you see these eels? Fresher than the day they were born—and fat as priests. I know where their burrows are, and I know what they like for bait. And as for frogs—I've been catching frogs since I was two years old; there's not a frog in Christendom jumps fast enough to get away from me—and I can swim as fast as any boy—and better than Drogo, the tanner!

Do you know Drogo, the tanner's apprentice? I can't point him out to you, because he'd see me. He's always staring at me. Many's the time I've seen him peel off his hose to show me his legs — as if every frog I've ever put into a pie didn't have better legs than his!

We had a brawl last summer. I said 'twas the fault of the tanners that the river stank, and he said 'twas the fishmongers. Which is pure folly: 'tis surely God's will that fish should rot in the water, but the beasts should rot on the land. I put out my tongue, and by Saint Peter,[4] he pushed me right off the wharf into the water. And then, poor fool, he thought I would drown — I, who couldn't drown when I was three hours old! He splashed in after me, and I dove down deep and grabbed his foot — and I ducked him three times, and serve him right. Only then I had to drag him out of the water — because it turns out, he can't swim! So I suppose you could say I saved his life.

He's never forgotten it. He watches me all the time — and shows off his legs. But I don't speak to him; I want nothing to do with him and his legs. I pretend I don't even know his name — and every day I walk past the tannery, just so he can see me not looking his way.

DROGO
THE TANNER'S APPRENTICE

I don't mind the stink—
    I grew up with it, being the son of a butcher.
    Dead things stink; that's the will of God,
        and tanners[1] make good money.

I don't mind the work—
    digging the pits
    grinding the oak bark
    smearing the hides with dung.
Work is work. I like
    bread in my belly
    and ale in my cup.

I do mind the jeering
    of Nelly the sniggler—
    her tongue could scrape the hair off a hide!
And I mind the townsmen
    nattering on,
    saying we foul the waters.[2]
By Saint Bartholomew,[3] think'st thou
    a man can make leather without filth?
    Alum, lime, oak galls, urine,
    ashes, tallow, and stale beer—
these are the tools of my trade.

Would you warm your hands in leather gloves?
　　Saddle or bridle your horse?
Do you dance to the sound of the bagpipes,
or lace up the cords of your armor?
What about the bellows, heating the forge?
　　It's leather—stinking leather!

Do you want good shoes or don't you?

So be it.
Now, let me get on with my scraper and dung.
You hold your nostrils—and hold your tongue.

GILES
THE BEGGAR

Good masters, sweet ladies!
    I am Giles the beggar,
        the best of my trade!
Behold my crushed foot!
    The sight of the wound
        would sicken your stomach, and soften your heart.
        A penny? A farthing?
        I grovel for mercy —
sometimes I manage real tears.
        (It's an art.)

No takers? No givers?
    Not even a morsel?
    Ah! They are stone to my pitiful cries.
And so I am left to my wits, which in fact
are prodigiously keen and surpassingly wise:

I enter a town, with my crutch and my cry:
    "Food for the famished! Alms for the poor!"
    I stagger, collapse in the dust of the road!
    I swoon — too exhausted to go one step more —

and here comes my father! (But I do not know him.)
    I lie by the roadside, starting to wail.

My father, the peddler, the dealer in relics:[1]
"Ten pence for a thread from Saint Margaret's veil!
Who covets the thumbnail of Martin of Tours?
Or this—better still—even this can be yours!

A flask of the healing holy water—
stand back, now—don't push, don't jostle—
    flask of the sacred holy water
        used on the feet of Saint James, Apostle!"

Sometimes they pay. More often they don't
    so he throws up his hands and he sighs—like that.
"Oh, ye of no faith! Before you, I swear
I will cure, here and now, this unfortunate brat!"

That's my cue. So I whimper.
He opens the flask,
    anoints me, while I seem to faint,
    with the authentic holy water
    used on the feet of the holy saint.
I swoon in his arms. Look upward! Cry out!
(Now see how the peasants step forward and gawk.)
    "Angels! Apostles! I see them before me!"
    I throw down my crutch, clasp my hands, and I *walk*!
    (My father and I
        rehearsed this for hours—
        miracles have to look perfectly natural.)
"He walks! Praise God and His saints! He walks!"

If I do it just right,
    the crowd gasps aloud—

they genuflect, weep,
    stretch their hands out, and touch.
And while they are paying
    for drops of that water,
    I gather my bandages,
    pick up my crutch.
My pantomime's done
    once the money is paid.
    I creep out of town.
    I feel guilt —
        but not much.

Later my father
    follows the highroad.
We meet, and he gives me
    my supper, my pay:
bread or an apple,
cabbages, turnips —
sometimes there's sausages
    on a good day.

We sup by the road,
    ask Our Lord to look after us:
    "Send us more fools
    for our food and our keep.
    Forgive us our trespasses,
    pardon our lies;
    look after your foxes
    as well as your sheep."

HUGO
THE LORD'S NEPHEW

[1] The Feast of All Souls, celebrated on November 2, is a holy day in honor of the dead.

[2] Friants are boar droppings.

[3] However the actor feels about kidneys and fat, this line should be spoken with enthusiasm. In the Middle Ages, it was difficult to get enough protein and fat in the diet. The kidneys of the boar would be a real treat.

TAGGOT
THE BLACKSMITH'S DAUGHTER

[1] May Day was an important medieval holiday. People celebrated by gathering flowers, dancing, flirting, and playing games.

[2] Many medieval children died young. Medieval mothers knew that they were unlikely to see all their children grow to adulthood.

[3] Most blacksmiths were men. However, a surprising number of medieval wives and daughters learned "masculine" trades, such as the art of the forge. Since many guilds were closed to women, these women were taught by their husbands or fathers.

[4] Though a farthing is only one quarter of a cent, Hugo is not being miserly. A full set of horseshoes would cost a penny.

ALICE
THE SHEPHERDESS

[1] The belief that sheep are fond of music is still with us today. Medieval shepherds used bagpipes to serenade their flocks.

[2] Alice sings her song to the melody of *"Edi beo thu"* written to the Virgin Mary.

[3] This is a true story, but it happened in the twentieth century. A farmer consoled a dying sheep by playing her guitar and singing through the night. The sheep recovered.

THOMAS
THE DOCTOR'S SON

[1] An egg white makes a good dressing because it's relatively sterile. Comfrey is still used to treat cuts and bruises.

[2] The five kinds of fever were hectic, pestilential, daily or quotidian, tertian, and quartan. Fevers were classified according to how often they recurred.

[3] The four humors—associated with the four elements of earth, air, fire, and water—were melancholic (cold and dry), sanguine (hot and moist), choleric (hot and dry), and phlegmatic (cold and moist). Good health depended on keeping these four humors in balance.

[4] Doctors knew astrology and believed that the stars could influence the well-being of their patients.

CONSTANCE
THE PILGRIM

[1] Constance's impulse to hide inside her cloak is entirely reasonable. In the Middle Ages, a deformity was considered a sign of God's displeasure.

[2] *Fell* is an old-fashioned word for ugly and bitter.

[3] *Caradog* is pronounced "kerr-ADD-ock." If you can roll the *r,* so much the better.

[4] To die unshriven is to die without confessing one's sins to a priest. Since Caradog dies directly after committing a mortal sin, there is little doubt about where he'll spend the afterlife.

MOGG
THE VILLEIN'S DAUGHTER

[1] A villein was a peasant who wasn't free. He could be bought and sold like a slave. His house, his family, and his labor all belonged to the lord of the manor.

[2] Mogg's chickens suffered from "gapes," caused by roundworms. The roundworms block the trachea, so infected birds look as if they're choking to death.

[3] On "can't lift his hand," the actress playing Mogg should lift her fist, so we know what kind of hand lifting she fears. Mogg's father is violent.

⁴ Villeins were bound by law to grind their grain at the lord's mill. The lord was entitled to a share of their grain or a small sum of money for the grinding.

⁵ Heriot, as Mogg tells us, was a widespread medieval custom. When a villein died, the lord had the right to his most valuable piece of livestock.

OTHO
THE MILLER'S SON

¹ Millers were unpopular men. The diet of medieval peasants was composed largely of bread. If the miller was dishonest, the peasants had less to eat, and no way to fight back, since grinding grain at home was against the law.

² Millers and bakers had all sorts of tricks to cheat the villein of his daily bread. Adulterating the flour with chalk was one.

³ The miller was socially superior to peasants and villeins, but greatly inferior to the lord. A miller's son like Otho was in an odd position—far beneath the children of nobility, but too "good" to play with common children.

⁴ The lord's demesne (pronounced "dim-MAIN") consisted of all his lands, including his strips in the three village fields. Since these strips of land ran alongside the strips belonging to the peasants, peasants were sometimes tempted to move the boundary stones in order to reap part of the lord's harvest.

SIMON
THE KNIGHT'S SON

[1] Richard the Lion-Heart fought in the Third Crusade, which lasted from 1189 to 1192. Richard did not, in fact, "save" the Holy City, but he did gain access to the Holy Sepulcher, the cave where Jesus was said to have been buried.

[2] If a man of the military or ruling class ran out of money, he couldn't just take up farming or making shoes—this would be too far to fall in the world. Simon could be a monk without losing his status as a nobleman.

[3] Simon the Monk would have to pray a minimum of seven times a day. Nevertheless, I think he is exaggerating.

EDGAR
THE FALCONER'S SON

[1] The sparrowhawk is a bird of prey, about the size of a small crow. Though sparrowhawks were easily obtained and inexpensive, they were difficult to tame.

[2] Prime was a church service held near dawn.

[3] The mews were a sort of stable where hunting birds were housed.

[4] Saint John's should be pronounced in the English way: "SIN-jinns." The sport of hawking was popular among monks and nuns, which is why Simon would be allowed to keep his bird in the abbey mews.

5 In the early stages of taming a bird, the bird's eyelids were "seeled"—sewn shut. This was said to calm the bird (it wouldn't calm me).

6 The word *callow* is actually a term from falconry. It refers to a nestling—Edgar is saying that Simon is immature.

ISOBEL
THE LORD'S DAUGHTER

1 These were all remedies for stain removal in the Middle Ages.

2 The duties of a lady included giving alms to poor people and loaves of bread on Lammas Day. Lammas was celebrated on August 1. In pagan times it was a celebration of the harvest. Later it became a feast day in honor of Saint Peter.

3 Isobel believes that her social status—and the status of those beneath her—is the will of God. This belief was both fostered and questioned by the Christian church.

BARBARY
THE MUD SLINGER

1 Many women died in childbirth, so it was not unusual for a man to marry three or four times.

2 The part of town where butchers, tanners, and fishmongers sold their wares was often called the Shambles or Shamble Lane. Originally *shamble* meant a slaughterhouse.

Jacob Ben Salomon
The Moneylender's Son and
Petronella
The Merchant's Daughter

[1] Jews had to identify themselves by wearing a yellow badge.

[2] Nones is about three o'clock in the afternoon. The church bells would ring to tell people that there was a prayer service at that time.

[3] There is no pause in the line "I never told a living soul." It should be spoken in one breath.

Lowdy
The Varlet's Child

[1] *Varlet* has come to mean a scoundrel, but in the Middle Ages it referred to a man who looked after animals.

[2] Pottage is a sort of stew. Poor people just threw whatever they had into the pot and hoped for the best.

[3] When Lowdy says that the house is hers to "keep," she's not saying that she's going to inherit it. "To keep house" is to make sure that the house is clean and tidy.

[4] *Brach* should be pronounced to rhyme with *thatch*. It seems to refer both to a hunting dog with a strong sense of smell and to a female dog; the word *dog* referred only to male dogs.

PASK
THE RUNAWAY

[1] The people of the Middle Ages didn't use our months of January, February, et cetera, but marked time by the feast days of the church.

PIERS
THE GLASSBLOWER'S
APPRENTICE

[1] According to tradition, Saint Luke once painted a portrait of the Virgin Mary, which made him the patron saint of all artists, including glass workers.

MARIOT AND MAUD
THE GLASSBLOWER'S
DAUGHTERS

[1] When Maud says that Piers is lousy, she's not using modern slang; she means he has body lice. Since clean clothes and frequent washing are necessary to banish these pests, it's likely that Maud has them, too.

NELLY
THE SNIGGLER

[1] Newborn babies have strong fingers and an instinct to hold on. The story about a baby catching hold of the bucket in which her father meant to drown her is true. The original plucky newborn was a woman named Liafburga, who lived around 700 A.D. (G.G. Coulton, *The Medieval Village*)

[2] Queen Eleanor of Aquitaine (1122–1204) was a legend in her own time.

[3] A sniggler is a person who catches eels by dangling bait into their holes in the riverbank. Frogs and eels were desirable sources of protein during the Middle Ages.

[4] Saint Peter was the patron saint of fishermen.

DROGO
THE TANNER'S APPRENTICE

[1] A tanner is someone who cures animal hides to make leather.

[2] Polluted waters are not just a contemporary problem. Almost everything that tanners used was poisonous. People like fishermen and brewers, who needed the rivers to be clean, were always at war with the tanners.

[3] Saint Bartholomew, who was skinned to death, was the patron saint of tanners. The logic of this is macabre, but not unique. Saint Sebastian, who was shot full of arrows, is the patron saint of archers; Saint Laurence, who was roasted alive, is the patron saint of cooks. We won't even talk about what happened to Saint Erasmus — it's too disgusting.

GILES
THE BEGGAR

[1] People of the Middle Ages were fascinated by relics. Most people believed that a fragment from a saint's body could work miracles.

BIBLIOGRAPHY

Ackerman, Diane. *A Natural History of Love*. New York: Random House, 1996.

Aries, Philippe, and Georges Duby. *A History of Private Life: Revelations of the Medieval World*. Cambridge, Mass.: Belknap Press/Harvard University Press, 1988.

Bagley, J. J. *Life in Medieval England*. New York: G. P. Putnam's Sons, 1960.

Bayard, Tania, translator and editor. *A Medieval Home Companion: Housekeeping in the Fourteenth Century*. New York: HarperPerennial, 1991.

Bishop, Morris. *The Middle Ages*. New York: American Heritage Press, 1986.

Bradley, Carolyn G. *Western World Costume: An Outline History*. New York: Prentice Hall, 1954.

Burke, John. *Life in the Castle in Medieval England*. London: B. T. Batsford Ltd., 1978.

Burrell, Roy. *The Middle Ages*. Oxford Junior History. Oxford: Oxford University Press, 1980.

Cairns, Trevor. *Medieval Knights*. Cambridge, England: Cambridge University Press, 1993.

——. *The Middle Ages*. Cambridge, England: Cambridge University Press, 1973.

Chaucer, Geoffrey. *Canterbury Tales*. Translated into Modern English by Nevill Coghill. Harmondsworth, Middlesex, England: Penguin Books, 2000.

Clare, Jon D. *Fourteenth Century Towns*. San Diego: Gulliver Books/ Harcourt Brace, 1993.

Clark, Kenneth. *Civilization: A Personal View*. New York: HarperCollins, 1990.

Compact Edition of the Oxford English Dictionary. Oxford: Oxford University Press, 1971.

Cootes, R. J. *The Middle Ages*. England: Longman Group Ltd., 1988.

Cosman, Madeleine Pelner. *Fabulous Feasts: Medieval Cookery and Ceremony*. New York: George Braziller, 1976.

Coulton, G. G. *The Medieval Village*. New York: Dover Publications, 1989.

Craft, Ruth. *Pieter Brueghel's The Fair*. Philadelphia: J. B. Lippincott Company, 1976.

Cresswell, Julia. *Tuttle Dictionary of First Names*. Boston: Charles E. Tuttle Company, 1992.

Cummins, John. *The Hound and the Hawk: The Art of Medieval Hunting*. New York: Palgrave MacMillan, 1988.

Davies, Penelope. *Growing Up in the Middle Ages*. Wayland, East Sussex, England: Main Line Book Co., 1972.

Duke, Dulcie. *Lincoln: The Growth of a Medieval Town*. Cambridge, England: Cambridge University Press, 1988.

Evans, Ivor H. *Brewer's Dictionary of Phrase and Fable*. New York: HarperCollins, 1989.

Fremantle, Anne. *Age of Faith*. Alexandria, Va.: Time-Life Books, 1966.

Gibb, Christopher. *Richard the Lionheart and the Crusades*. East Sussex, England: Watts, 1985.

Gies, Frances, and Joseph Gies. *Cathedral, Forge and Waterwheel: Technology and Invention in the Middle Ages*. New York: HarperCollins, 1994.

———. *Daily Life in Medieval Times*. New York: Black Dog and Leventhal Publishers, 1999.

——. *Women in the Middle Ages.* New York: Thomas Y. Crowell Co., 1978.

Gimpel, Jean. *The Medieval Machine: The Industrial Revolution of the Middle Ages.* London: Viking Penguin, 1977.

Hanawalt, Barbara A. *Growing Up in Medieval London: The Experience of Childhood in History.* New York: Oxford University Press, 1995.

Hartman, Gertrude. *Medieval Days and Ways.* New York: Atheneum, 1967.

Herlihy, David. *Medieval Households.* Cambridge, Mass.: Harvard University Press, 1985.

Hirn, Yrjo. *The Sacred Shrine.* Boston: Beacon Press, 1957.

Hughes, Dom Anselm. *Early Medieval Music up to 1300.* London: Oxford University Press, 1955.

James, Peter, and Nick Thorpe. *Ancient Inventions.* New York: Ballantine Books, 1995.

Jones, Evan, and Judith Jones. *The Book of Bread.* New York: HarperCollins, 1986.

Knopf Guides. *Venice.* New York: Alfred A. Knopf, 1993.

Labarge, Margaret Wade. *A Small Sound of the Trumpet: Women in Medieval Life.* Boston: Beacon Press, 1988.

Laing, Lloyd, and Jennifer Laing. *Medieval Britain: The Age of Chivalry.* New York: Palgrave MacMillan, 1996.

Morgan, Gwyneth. *Life in a Medieval Village.* Cambridge, England: Cambridge University Press, 1975.

Power, Eileen. *Medieval Women.* Cambridge, England: Cambridge University Press, 1997.

Reader's Digest. *Everyday Life Through the Ages.* New York: Reader's Digest Association, 1992.

Reeves, Marjorie. *The Medieval Town*. London: Addison-Wesley, 1954.

Sancha, Sheila. *The Luttrell Village: Country Life in the Middle Ages*. New York: Thomas Y. Crowell, 1983.

——. *Walter Dragon's Town: Crafts and Trade in the Middle Ages*. New York: Lippincott and Williams & Wilkins Publishers, 1989.

Sargent, Brian. *Minstrels: Medieval Music to Sing and Play*. Cambridge, England: Cambridge University Press, 1974.

Simons, Gerald. *Barbarian Europe*. Alexandria, Va: Time-Life Books, 1968.

Singman, Jeffrey L., and Will McLean. *Daily Life in Chaucer's England*. Westport, Conn.: Greenwood Press, 1995.

Smith, Lesley M., editor. *The Making of Britain: The Middle Ages*. London Weekend Television. London: Schocken Books, 1985.

Thie, Greg. *Living in the Past: The Middle Ages*. Oxford: Basil Blackwell, 1983.

Walsh, Michael, editor. *Butler's Lives of the Saints*. Concise Edition, Revised and Updated. San Francisco: Harper San Francisco, 1991.

Wilkins, Frances. *Growing Up During the Norman Conquest*. London: David & Charles, 1980.

Wilkinson, Philip, and Jacqueline Dineen. *The Early Inventions*. New York: Chelsea House, 1995.

Withycombe, E. G. *The Oxford Dictionary of English Christian Names*. Oxford: Oxford University Press, 1986.

LAURA AMY SCHLITZ has spent most of her life working as a librarian and professional storyteller. She has also been a playwright, a costumer, and an actress, and her plays for young people have been produced in professional theaters all over the country. She wrote the pieces in this book for a group of students at the Park School in Baltimore, where she works. As she explains, "They were studying the Middle Ages and were going at it hammer and tongs. I wanted them to have something to perform, but no one wanted a small part. So I decided to write several monologues instead of one long play, so that for three minutes at least, every child could be a star." Laura Amy Schlitz is also the author of *The Hero Schliemann: The Dreamer Who Dug for Troy,* a biography illustrated by Robert Byrd; *A Drowned Maiden's Hair: A Melodrama; Bearskinner: A Tale of the Brothers Grimm,* illustrated by Max Grafe; and *The Night Fairy,* a novel for young readers illustrated in full-color by Angela Barrett.

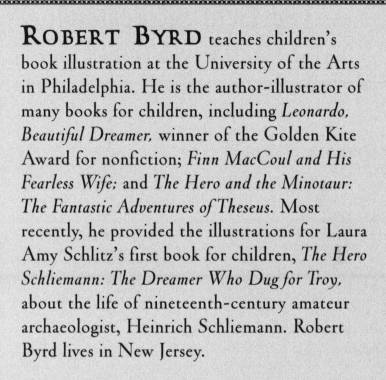

ROBERT BYRD teaches children's book illustration at the University of the Arts in Philadelphia. He is the author-illustrator of many books for children, including *Leonardo, Beautiful Dreamer,* winner of the Golden Kite Award for nonfiction; *Finn MacCoul and His Fearless Wife;* and *The Hero and the Minotaur: The Fantastic Adventures of Theseus.* Most recently, he provided the illustrations for Laura Amy Schlitz's first book for children, *The Hero Schliemann: The Dreamer Who Dug for Troy,* about the life of nineteenth-century amateur archaeologist, Heinrich Schliemann. Robert Byrd lives in New Jersey.

ALSO BY LAURA AMY SCHLITZ, ILLUSTRATED BY ROBERT BYRD

The Hero Schliemann:
The Dreamer Who Dug for Troy

AGES 9–13 · GRADES 4–8
HARDCOVER ISBN: 978-0-7636-2283-1

A *Bulletin of the Center for Children's Books* Blue Ribbon Winner

A Junior Library Guild Selection

"Schlitz's chatty text is frank with the reader about the difficulties of parsing fact from Schliemann's fiction. . . . Byrd's wry illustrations match the breeziness of the text and add verve to the whole."
— *Kirkus Reviews*

★ "Anyone with an interest in archaeology or in liars and braggarts will be drawn in by this slim biography of the hyperimaginative Schliemann.'
— *Bulletin of the Center for Children's Books* (starred review)

"This intriguing, well-documented biography is made more compelling by information boxes on history and such literary figures as Homer. Byrd's ink-and-watercolor illustrations . . . add to this captivating story."
— *School Library Journal*

The Bearskinner:
A Tale of the Brothers Grimm

illustrated by Max Grafe

AGES 8–11 · GRADES 3–6
HARDCOVER ISBN: 978-0-7636-2730-0

An American Library
Association Notable
Children's Book

A *Horn Book*
Fanfare Selection

★ "An unabashedly old-fashioned retelling, making few concessions to modern sensibilities; as such, it carries a power rarely found in fairy-tale retellings."
—*Kirkus Reviews* (starred review)

★ "Schlitz narrates with clarity, grace, and sensitivity. . . . A provocative edition that should set older children thinking about the meaning of endurance and heroism." —*The Horn Book* (starred review)

A Drowned Maiden's Hair:
A Melodrama

A CYBIL Award winner

A *Bulletin of the Center for Children's Books* Blue Ribbon Winner

A *Horn Book* Fanfare Selection

A Junior Library Guild Selection

AGES 10–14 · GRADES 5–9
HARDCOVER ISBN: 978-0-7636-2930-4
PAPERBACK ISBN: 978-0-7636-3812-2
E-BOOK ISBN: 978-0-7636-5215-9

★ "Schlitz realizes both characters and setting . . . with unerring facility."
—*The Horn Book* (starred review)

"The details and the surprising turnarounds will keep readers hooked."
—*Booklist*

"Exciting, intriguing, and, above all, the story is entrancing."
—*School Library Journal*

"Delightful. . . . A fascinating look into the sham underside of turn-of-the-century spiritualism." —*The New York Times Book Review*

Visit www.candlewick.com to download a Teachers' Guide for

Good Masters! Sweet Ladies!
Voices from a Medieval Village

The teachers' guide was prepared by Ellen Myrick, who studied the Middle Ages at the University of Manchester, in England, and has written teachers' guides for Avi's *Crispin: The Cross of Lead; Crispin: At the Edge of the World;* and *The Book Without Words.*

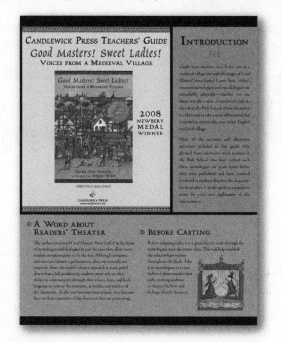

The Night Fairy

illustrated by Angela Barrett

An Amazon.com
Best Book of the Year

A *Booklist* Top Ten Science
Fiction/Fantasy Novel
For Youth

An IndieBound Kids'
Next List Selection

AGES 7–11 · GRADES 2–6
HARDCOVER ISBN: 978-0-7636-3674-6
PAPERBACK ISBN: 978-0-7636-5295-1
E-BOOK ISBN: 978-0-7636-5439-9

★ "An imaginative adventure story in a familiar, yet exotic landscape. . . .
Beautifully composed, the artwork combines subtle use of color with a keen
observation of nature that's reminiscent of Beatrix Potter's work. This finely
crafted and unusually dynamic fairy story is a natural for reading aloud."
— *Booklist* (starred review)

★ "Beautifully crafted. . . . Barrett's full-color watercolor illustrations add depth
and perspective to the story. Sure to be a favorite among girls who love fairies."
— *School Library Journal* (starred review)

"This elegant hardback's snug size and Angela Barrett's exquisite miniature
illustrations have the effect of making readers feel as if they've crept through
a magic portal into a fairy-scale world. Indeed, looking up at story's end,
children may be mildly surprised to find that they're still the size they've
always been." — *The Wall Street Journal*